Madeline Finn
and the
Library Dog

For all my furry friends and those who love them, thank you.
And for libraries, where the real magic happens.

—L. P.

AN OLD BARN BOOK

Text and illustrations Copyright © 2016 by Lisa Papp

Published in 2017 in the UK and Australia and New Zealand
by Old Barn Books Ltd, Warren Barn, West Sussex, RH20 1JW, UK
This paperback edition first published in 2018 by Old Barn Books
www.oldbarnbooks.com

First published in the United States under the title
MADELINE FINN AND THE LIBRARY DOG by Lisa Papp.
Published by arrangement with Peachtree Publishers.
Edited by Kathy Landwehr
Design and composition by Nicola Simmonds Carmack
The illustrations were rendered in pencil, watercolour and digital colouring

Distributed in the UK by Bounce Sales & Marketing
and in Australia and New Zealand by Walker Books Australia

ISBN 978-1-910646-33-5

10 9 8 7 6 5 4 3 2 1

Printed in Malaysia by Tien Wah Press

MIX
Paper from responsible sources
FSC
www.fsc.org
FSC® C012700

Paper in this book is certified against the
Forest Stewardship Council® standards.
FSC® promotes environmentally responsible,
socially beneficial and economically viable
management of the world's forests.

Madeline Finn
and the
Library Dog

Lisa Papp

Old Barn Books

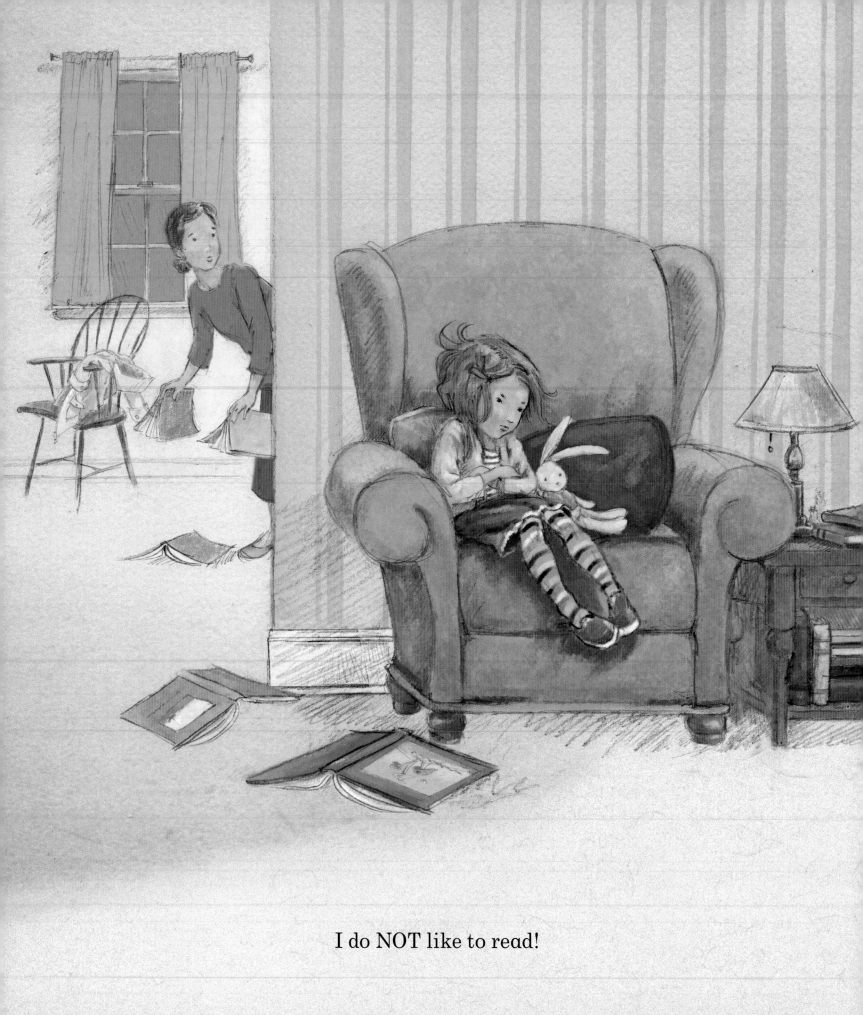

I do NOT like to read!

Not books.

Not magazines.

Not even the menu on the

ice cream van.

And I ESPECIALLY do not like to read out loud.

"Keep trying, Madeline Finn," my teacher says.

But sometimes I can't figure out the words.

Sometimes the sentences get stuck in my mouth like peanut butter.

Sometimes people giggle when I make a mistake.

And I never get a star sticker from my teacher.

Not even a smiley face.

Instead, I get a heart that says Keep Trying.

I get a lot of Keep Trying stickers.

But I want the star.

Stars are for good readers.

Stars are for understanding words,

and for saying them out loud.

But I know what else they're for.

Stars are for making wishes!

So I make a wish for my very own star.

I guess wishes take a while, because I don't get my star

on Monday or Tuesday.

"Keep trying," my teacher tells me on Wednesday.

On Thursday, I say the frog's name wrong. It's Samuel.

I try to get away with Sam, but it doesn't work.

Friday is no better.

On Saturday, Mum takes me to the library.

"Hello, Madeline Finn," Mrs. Dimple says.

She's our librarian.

"I don't like to read," I remind her, in case she forgot.

"Oh, I remember," she says. "But today we have

something special—something you might enjoy."

"Madeline Finn, would you like to read to a dog?"

Mrs. Dimple leads me over to a big white dog.
"This is Bonnie. Why don't you pick out a book to
read to her? She's a great listener."

Bonnie is beautiful. Like a big, snowy polar bear.

"Would you like to try?" Mum asks.

"Yes please," I say. (But not very loud.)

At first, I'm nervous.

I get the letters mixed up.

The words don't sound right.

But then I look at Bonnie, and she looks right
into my eyes. She doesn't giggle.

I feel better. I try again.

Halfway through, I get stuck on another word.

Bonnie doesn't mind. She puts her big paws in

my lap and lets me stroke her until I figure it out.

After that, Bonnie and I read

together every Saturday.

It's fun to read when you're not afraid of
making mistakes. Bonnie teaches me that it's
okay to go slow, and to keep trying—just like
the sticker says.

I still don't have a star.

But I can be patient.

Like Bonnie.

Soon, it's almost time to read in class again. But when I go to the library, Bonnie's not there! Neither is Mrs. Dimple.

"Would you like to wait for another dog?" the other librarian asks.

"No thank you," I say, as politely as I can.

"Don't worry," Mum tells me later.

"Bonnie was just busy today."

"But what about school?" I ask.

"You'll do fine," she says. "Just pretend

you're reading to Bonnie."

On Monday morning, I am very nervous.

"Madeline Finn, would you like to read next?" the teacher asks.

"Yes, please," I say. (But still not very loud.)

The first sentence goes pretty well. Then I mess up on a word.

And then another. I hear someone giggle.

But then I think about Bonnie. I take a deep breath and pretend she's right next to me.

Next thing I know, I'm at the bottom of the page.

I look at my teacher and she has a big smile on her face.

I did it! I got my star!

On Saturday, we go to the library again. Mrs. Dimple is back!

"I got my star!" I tell her. "I want to give it to Bonnie."

"Well done, Madeline Finn!" she says.

"I think Bonnie might have a surprise

for you too."

"Madeline Finn, would you like to read to Bonnie—and her puppies?"

"Yes, please!" I say, nice and loud.